And the crocodile snapped,
and the tiger growled,

The lion roared
and the monkeys howled,

The elephant trumpeted —
trump, trump, trump!

"Humph," said the camel
with the great big hump.

The hyena laughed and
the hummingbird whirred,

But the ladybird
said never a word.

But the ladybird saw, and the ladybird heard . . .

She saw two men she already knew.
They were Lanky Len and Hefty Hugh,
And she heard them chuckle, "Ho ho ho!
We're going to kidnap Monkey Joe."

"We'll hide till there's no one else about,
Then we'll pick the lock and we'll get Joe out,
And if we give him lots of fruit
He'll do the job and he'll get the loot.
The palace isn't far at all.
Monkey Joe can scale the wall.

He'll find out where the Queen's asleep,
Then – tiptoe – into her room he'll creep.
He'll open the sack and steal the crown.
We'll soon be the richest men in town!"

The little spotty ladybird
Told the animals what she'd heard.

And the crocodile snapped, and the tiger growled,
The lion roared and the monkeys howled,
The elephant trumpeted — trump, trump, trump!
"Humph," said the camel with the great big hump.
The hyena cried and the hummingbird whirred,
And all of the animals, feathered and furred,
Said, "No no no! NO NO NO!
We can't let them kidnap Monkey Joe!"

But the ladybird had a good idea
And she whispered it into the monkey's ear.

Then straight away, the ladybird
Flew to the palace, and had a word
With the Queen's two corgis, Willow and Holly,
And one said, "Gosh!" and the other said, "Golly!"

And both the dogs agreed to do
Just what the ladybird told them to.

At dead of night the two bad men,
Hefty Hugh and Lanky Len,
Checked there was no one else about,
Then they picked the lock and they got Joe out.

They carried him off to the palace gate,
Gave him a sack, then lay in wait.
They watched him scale the palace wall,
And they muttered, "Careful not to fall!"

Then they rubbed their hands as they saw him creeping
Into the room where the Queen lay sleeping.

Corgi Holly and Corgi Willow,
Who lay each side of the Queen's soft pillow,
Were wide awake, and they said to Joe,
"Come on, Monkey – off we go."

They led the way while the Queen still slept,
And they showed young Joe where their bones were kept.
Then they helped the monkey fill the sack
And they wagged their tails as he carried it back.

The two thieves yelled, "Hip hip hooray!
But now let's make our getaway."

They carried the sack to a nice quiet park
Where the only sound was a distant bark.
They found a bench and both sat down,
And Hugh said, "Time to see that crown!"
"I just can't wait," said Lanky Len.
They opened up the sack, but then . . .

You should have heard their moans and groans,
To find the sack was full of bones!

Just then, a dog came bounding up,
And Hugh said, "Shoo, you greedy pup!"
Another dog was close behind,
And then came dogs of every kind.

A lurcher and a Labrador,
A Peke, a pug, then more and more.
Black dogs, white dogs, grey and brown –
It seemed like every dog in town.

They seized the bones, and gnashed and gnawed,
Tugged and tussled, pawed and clawed,
Then turned upon the robbers, yelping,
"How about a second helping?"

The thieves took off, with leaps and bounds,
Pursued by all the hungry hounds,
While the monkey ran and the ladybird flew
With never a stop till they reached the zoo.

Then the crocodile grinned, and the tiger pranced,
The lion leapt and the monkeys danced,
The elephant trumpeted — trump, trump, trump!
"Hooray!" said the camel with the great big hump.
The hyena laughed and the hummingbird whirred,

But the ladybird said never a word.

For Willow and in memory
of Holly, the Queen's corgis

First published 2017 by Macmillan Children's Books
This edition published 2021 by Macmillan Children's Books
an imprint of Pan Macmillan
The Smithson, 6 Briset Street, London EC1M 5NR
Associated companies throughout the world.
www.panmacmillan.com

ISBN: 978-1-5290-5142-1

1 3 5 7 9 8 6 4 2

A CIP catalogue record for this book is available from the British Library.

Printed in China.